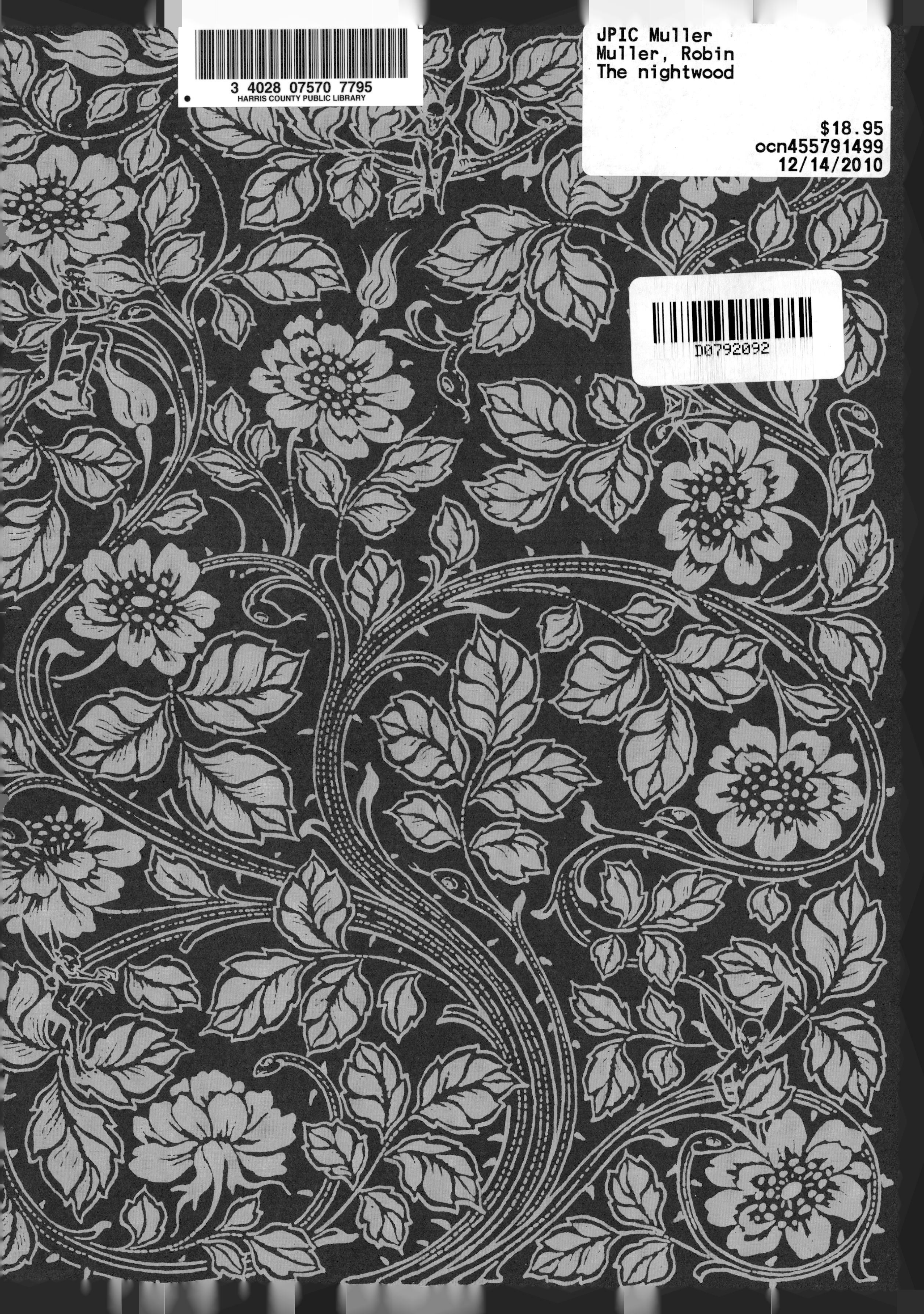

ROBIN MULLER

The Nightwood

TUNDRA BOOKS

To the lady in white at the foot of my bed.

Published in Canada by Tundra Books,
75 Sherbourne Street, Toronto, Ontario M5A 2P9

Published in the United States by Tundra Books of Northern New York,
P.O. Box 1030, Plattsburgh, New York 12901

First published in 1991 by Doubleday Canada

Library of Congress Control Number: 2009938449

Library and Archives Canada Cataloguing in Publication

Muller, Robin
The nightwood / Robin Muller.

Interest age level: For ages 5-8.
ISBN 978-1-77049-209-7

I. Title.

PS8576.U424N5 2009a jC813'.54 C2009-906017-5

We acknowledge the financial support of the Government of Canada through the Book Publishing Industry Development Program (BPIDP) and that of the Government of Ontario through the Ontario Media Development Corporation's Ontario Book Initiative. We further acknowledge the support of the Canada Council for the Arts and the Ontario Arts Council for our publishing program.

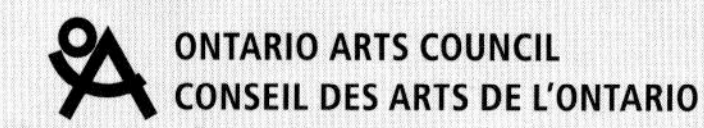

Design: Kong Njo
Printed and bound in Hong Kong

1 2 3 4 5 6 15 14 13 12 11 10

"Beware of the Elves
Who come in the night
To visit your dreams
And give you a fright.

"Beware of the Elves
And their magical Queen
Who turns joy to sorrow
And laughter to pain.

"Beware of the Elves.
All children must learn:
If you stray in the woods
You may never return."

LONG AGO THERE STOOD A FOREST deep, green and beautiful. Sunlight danced along its paths, and birdsong filled its cool, leafy spaces.

One night a mist came rolling down from the north. Hidden in the silver gloom rode a strange, unearthly band. At its head was a spirit creature, wondrous and terrible to behold. Her skin was the color of fresh cream, but her eyes were as black as pitch. The mist and its riders passed over the countryside like a shadow, then came to rest in the very heart of the forest.

By dawn, thick clumps of briar had sprung up choking every glade and dell. Mocking voices echoed amongst the ancient trees coaxing travelers from their paths. Children, who played beneath the forest's boughs, were never seen again. Even brave knights, daring to explore the secrets of the wood, vanished. Only their empty armor was ever found, broken and pierced by thorns.

As time passed, the branches of the trees grew so tangled that no daylight could penetrate its depths. The forest was given a new name: the Nightwood. For leagues around, people were warned never to go there, for the forest had become the home of the dreaded Elfin Queen.

NEAR THE NIGHTWOOD stood a castle, the home of the Earl of March and his daughter, Elaine.

A merrier maiden could not be found, always vexing her old nurse by dancing amongst the trees at the Nightwood's edge.

"You're as wild as the Earl of Roxborough's son," scolded the old woman. "He was warned about the Nightwood, but one moonlit night he strayed beneath its shadow and vanished. No one has seen hide nor hair of him for nearly seven years."

"Your nursery stories don't frighten me," teased Elaine. "But to stop your worrying, I'll sit still and practice my needlework and prove to you how good I can be!"

Elaine took up her needle and started to embroider the image of a handsome young knight. But as soon as the nurse busied herself with her tasks, Elaine let the needle slip and gazed out over the battlements toward the Nightwood.

ONE BRIGHT SPRING MORNING the Earl announced that there was to be a great ball in honor of a company of visiting knights.

"At last!" cried Elaine, "I shall attend a ball. I'll unbraid my hair, put on my prettiest gown, and dance till my slippers are in tatters!"

"You will do no such thing!" said her father sternly. "The company of knights is no place for a child."

"I'm not a child!" protested Elaine. "I'm a young woman – and I want to dance at the ball!" But her father was unmoved.

On the night of the festivities Elaine sat all alone. From her window she could see the Nightwood spreading like a dark sea under the moon's glow. As she gazed at the swaying treetops, lights, bright as shooting stars, flashed on the evening breeze, and voices from the shadows called to her, "Come and dance. Come and dance."

"I will come," answered Elaine. She wrapped her cloak around her and crept down the stairs.

THE HALL blazed with light as lords and ladies pranced in a noisy reel.

From where she hid, Elaine could hear her father telling a group of nobles how his child wanted to attend the ball. "Why," he laughed, "it was only yesterday that she was learning how to walk."

Elaine's heart burned with fury at his words. "The Elfin Queen is also holding a ball," she murmured. "If I cannot dance at my father's, then I will dance at hers."

Quietly Elaine pulled open the castle door and stole into the night.

Guided by the moon, Elaine made her way till the forest loomed before her, stern and black. As she stepped into its gloom, a hand shot out, seizing her wrist and pulling her back.

Elaine gasped as she looked into the face of a haggard old woman, "This is no place for a pretty young lass like you!" the woman hissed. "Leave now, while you can!"

"I won't!" cried Elaine, "I'm going to the Elfin Queen's ball, so let me go!" She broke free of the woman's grasp and dashed into the wood.

As Elaine raced forward, the gentle breeze turned into a fierce gale driving her along like a dry leaf. Thorns ripped her clothing, roots tripped her, and branches slashed her face. "Stop, please stop!" she cried as she tumbled to the ground. "I only want to join the ball."

As suddenly as it had begun, the wind ceased.

Elaine found herself in a small clearing bathed in moonlight. In front of her grew a rose bush like none she had ever seen. Each blossom shimmered in the night as if possessed of its own flame.

In wonder, Elaine got to her feet and approached the glowing bush. The blossoms seemed to pulse to the beating of her heart. She reached out, snapped a stem, and drank in the flower's fragrance.

"Who dares pick the favorite flower of the Elfin Queen?"

BEFORE HER STOOD a handsome youth, curiously dressed, with nine tinkling bells swinging from his belt.

"I dare," she said. "I am Elaine, daughter of the Earl of March, master of all these lands, including," she added haughtily, "this forest."

The youth laughed and made a low bow. "Pardon me, Earl of March's daughter. I had not expected such an important visitor. I am Tamlynne, matchless knight of the Elfin Queen. It is my duty to guard this bush against intruders. The flowers bloom only when the moon is full – and only by carrying one can a mortal enter and leave the Elfin land in safety. If the Queen knew you had plucked a rose, her anger would be terrible."

Tamlynne gazed at Elaine. "But I will not betray one so bold. How may I serve you?"

"I have come to attend the Elfin Queen's ball," Elaine replied. "Could you escort me?"

Tamlynne's smile vanished. "It is perilous for mortals to dance at an Elfin ball," he said slowly. "Even with the flower's protection, most mortals never return, and those who do, pine away, blind to the beauty of their own world."

"I am not afraid," cried Elaine. "If you do not take me, I shall find the ball myself!"

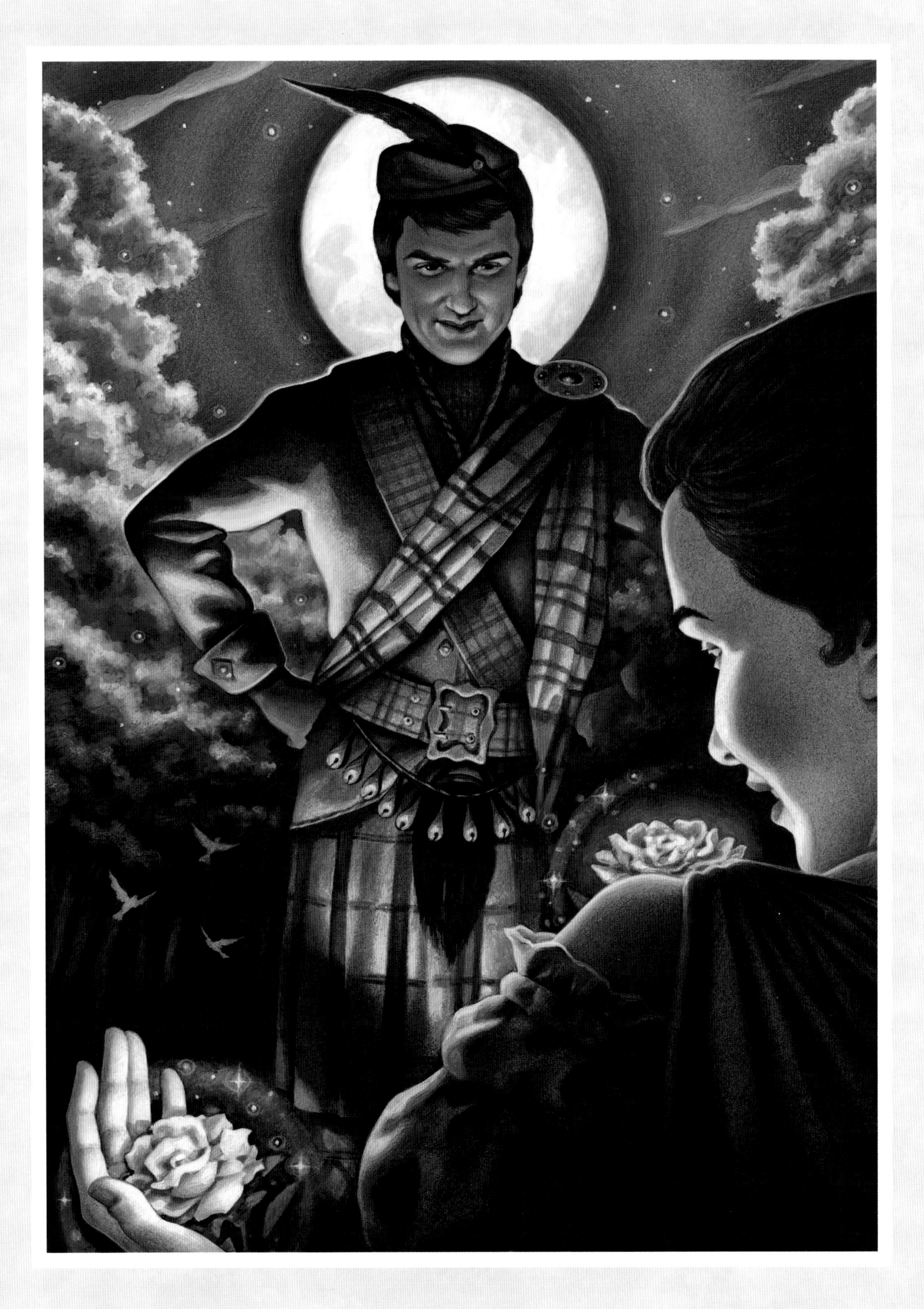

TAMLYNNE SIGHED, "If your heart is set upon it."

He took the blossom, gently blew on it, and placed it in her hair. Instantly the forest changed. Elaine found herself on a broad lawn. Music, stranger, wilder, and sweeter than she had ever heard before, rose and fell on the velvet air. The notes seemed to echo the soft pulse of the forest, the sighs of the wind in the trees, and the deep throbbing of underground rivers.

A youth and a maiden stepped into the clearing and floated gracefully round in a great circle. Soon others joined them, all gliding to a melody that seemed to swell from every tree and stone.

"Who are these dancers?" asked Elaine. "They move like people in a slumber."

"These were once mortal children," said Tamlynne sorrowfully. "Children who stole into the wood and fell under its enchantment. Children like you."

"I am not a child," cried Elaine. "And I am not afraid to dance. You said the flower would protect me, so dance with me!" She seized Tamlynne's arm and led him into the circle.

Elaine felt herself swept along between earth and sky. Never had she known such joy. On and on went the revels as though time had no end. Then, just as Elaine felt she might dance forever, the music came suddenly to a halt.

"YOU MUST GO," whispered Tamlynne. "The night is spent and you have visited a forbidden place. Farewell Elaine. Remember me!" He touched the flower in her hair and everything vanished. Only the gentle tinkling of the bells that Tamlynne wore at his waist hung in the air. Elaine found herself standing once more at the entrance to the wood.

"Visiting with elves?" said a voice in her ear. The old woman stood by her side. "Listening to their tales and dancing to their music?"

"And if I were?" said Elaine. "I am free to do as I wish – even dance if I choose to."

"Be warned, young lady," croaked the old woman. "The Elfin Queen does not like intruders. She has the power to drain them of life. If you're not careful you will become like that shrivelled flower in your hair!"

Elaine felt for the rose, but it was now withered, crumbling to dust at her touch.

Frightened by the change in the flower, Elaine turned and fled. The crone's voice pursued her as she ran, "Away, keep away. The cost of visiting here is great!"

THE NEXT DAY ELAINE'S old nurse entered her room, bursting with gossip from the night's festivities. Elaine did not hear a word. She was lost in a dream of the Nightwood and the young knight, Tamlynne. And so she remained for weeks.

On the next full moon, Elaine waited till all were asleep, then raced to the forest's edge. Gingerly she stepped between the trees, expecting the wind to assail her again. But the evening air was still. Patches of moonlight guided her to the clearing. The Nightwood had been waiting for her.

The bush stood before her, its blossoms softly glowing against the darkness. She plucked a rose, and instantly Tamlynne was beside her.

Through the night they danced, the stars spinning above their heads. Together they whirled amongst the dancers, the music lifting their feet. Then, at last, the dawn's rays tinged the sky and Elaine was alone.

◆

Through the spring and summer, every time the moon was full, Elaine visited the Nightwood. But with each visit there was a marked change in her appearance. She who had been the flower of her father's court, praised for her beauty and high spirits, now sat listless and withdrawn.

AROUND THE CASTLE frightened servants huddled together, whispering about Elaine. "She has been to the Nightwood. She has danced with the elves. That is why she is so pale. The Earl must not hear of this!"

But the secret could not be kept. When the Earl learned the truth he wept. "Lock her away," he cried. "Watch her day and night. We must keep her from the forest if we are to break this evil spell."

Elaine was locked in her room in the tower. Feverish dreams tumbled through her mind, dreams that the young knight she loved would be lost to her forever. "He's calling to me!" she would cry, and to some it did seem as if her name was carried, sad and low, on the evening breeze.

Summer passed into autumn. In the Nightwood chill winds swept through the trees, and leaves covered the ground like a golden carpet.

In the tower Elaine, too, had changed. She no longer called out for her love, and the color returned to her cheeks. "At last she seems to have forgotten her Elfin knight," the old nurse confided to all who enquired.

ONE NIGHT, when heavy clouds hid the full moon, Elaine called to her nurse: "Come and sit with me while I play." She took her lute and strummed an old lullaby her nurse loved to hear. Soon the old woman was asleep. Slipping the key from the nurse's pocket, Elaine unlocked the door, crept down the stairs, and disappeared into the night.

In the clearing, the rosebush that had always summoned Tamlynne stood in the cold darkness, bare of leaf and flower. "No!" cried Elaine. "They can't all have faded!" A bitter wind whistled through the trees, the clouds parted, and a single ray from the moon shone full and bright. Nestled at the heart of the bush was a dry, unopened bud. Elaine quickly plucked and kissed it. The warmth of her caress revived the bud, transforming it into a beautiful rose.

"I feared that you had forgotten me," said Tamlynne as he stepped from the shadows. "My heart broke at the thought we would never meet again."

Elaine told him of her imprisonment. "If only you were a mortal," she wept.

"I am a mortal," said Tamlynne. "I am the son of the Earl of Roxborough. One night while I was out riding, a terrible storm overtook me. Blinding rain and a great wind forced me from my path. A thunder crack startled my horse. She threw me and then bolted into the night. Bruised and weak, I took shelter in the forest. The Elfin Queen found me and made me a knight of her court. For almost seven years I have lived as in a dream. You have woken me. Now all I desire is to be at your side."

"Come with me then!" begged Elaine.

"I cannot," sighed Tamlynne, "I am under an enchantment. At the end of the seventh year, on All Hallow's Eve, my soul will be forfeit. For it is then that the Elfin Queen and her court have to leave the wood in search of a new home. When that happens all mortals caught in her web will become creatures of air, unable to laugh or cry or love – their voices nothing more than the sad, rustling murmur of the wind through the trees!"

SUDDENLY TAMLYNNE stiffened and, hiding the rose in a pocket in Elaine's cloak, pushed her behind him. Coming toward them was a beautiful lady, the loveliest Elaine had ever seen. It was the Elfin Queen.

"Who is this?" the Queen asked Tamlynne.

She smiled graciously when told that Elaine was the daughter of the Earl of March.

"You are most welcome, my dear, though it is late in the year if you have come to admire my roses. Still, we have other entertainments. You must come and join our ball." Taking them both by the arm, she led them away.

The lawn had changed. Where before it had shimmered with silvery light, like the arc of the new moon, now it was like a sunset, red as blood. Tamlynne put his arms around Elaine and held her tightly. Round and round they went. The dancers seemed caught in a windless storm, whirling and tossing like leaves. Elaine's heart shook as the dancers' voices were suddenly raised in song, deafening and terrible.

Then, without warning, the music fell into a shuddering gulf of silence. Once more Elaine found herself alone.

"It is not wise to love an Elfin knight," sighed the old woman as she stepped into the clearing.

"MY LOVE IS A MORTAL," cried Elaine tearfully. And she told her of Tamlynne's plight. "I must find a way to save him!"

"There is a way," replied the crone, "but one with a terrible cost."

"As a girl I lived in a kingdom far from here. I was wild and carefree and loved a lad with all my heart. But one night the Elfin Queen and her court stole into our country. For seven dreadful years, youths and maidens, including the one I loved, fell prey to her enchantments. I vowed to save him. On All Hallow's Eve, the night the Elfin court had to leave, I crept into the forest and tried to drag him away."

"The Elfin Queen's anger was terrible. Once he was in my arms she changed my love into a bucking stag, but I held on. Then he became a snarling wolf, but I would not let go. But then she turned him into a pillar of fire, scorching my flesh and choking me. I could hold him no more." Tears streamed from her eyes. "I released my hold and lost my love forever. Now I follow wherever they wander, warning those who would forget their own world to dance in the Elfin throng."

"Tomorrow night is All Hallow's Eve. Just before dawn the Elfin court will gather to leave the glade. To save Tamlynne you must find him and pull him from his horse. Do not let go of him, no matter what shape he may become, till the enchantment is broken."

"BUT BE WARNED," said the old woman. "If you succeed, the Queen's anger will be so great she will take your life in his stead. That is the cost! Only your heart knows if you are strong enough for such a trial."

The day passed, cold and dreary. Storm clouds hung low in the sky and an autumn drizzle cast a chill blanket on the countryside. Elaine sat alone in her room gazing pensively out at the gray pall covering the Nightwood. As evening fell, shutters were barred, doors bolted, and the castle grew still. Hour after hour Elaine sat motionless. Then, as the clock struck the hour before dawn, she threw on her cloak and hurried down the winding stairs, letting herself out into the darkness.

At the edge of the glade she hid herself and waited. As she did, the sky broke and the moon emerged from between the clouds. Suddenly the sound of hooves filled the night. The Elfin court had assembled.

In the half-light she could barely make out the riders. "How shall I find Tamlynne amongst so many?" she gasped. Then, dancing above the sound of the hooves, she caught the tinkle of bells, nine bells swinging at the waist of a knight riding beside the Elfin Queen.

"Tamlynne!" cried Elaine as she rushed forward and pulled the rider to the ground. There arose an unearthly cry: "Tamlynne's stolen away. Tamlynne's stolen away!"

ELAINE CLASPED TAMLYNNE to her in a fierce embrace. A ferocious bear, huge and hairy, was suddenly in her arms. It roared and twisted, trying to shake her off. Elaine held on. The bear vanished. She was clasping a terrified dove, beating her with its wings. The dove turned into a huge serpent, hissing and coiling its body around her. Elaine felt her hands slipping along its cold, waxy scales, but she would not let go. The serpent changed into a fiery brand burning into the very bones of her fingers. Elaine moaned with pain. Without letting go, she staggered to a pool at the edge of the clearing and thrust the brand into the icy water. The spell was broken: her arms were around Tamlynne once more.

The Elfin Queen's eyes blazed with rage. "You have stolen my knight," she screamed. "For that you will pay with your life!" The Queen raised her hand to strike the breath from the girl's body. But, at that moment, a sharp cry split the darkness as a cock's crow announced the first sweet rays of dawn.

"Away," cried the assembly. "We must away!"

"The dawn has cheated me," hissed the Queen. "Farewell, Tamlynne. I was foolish to think that no power was greater than the Queen of the Elves. I was wrong. The power of mortal love is greater!"

WITH A WAVE OF HER HAND the Elfin Queen and her followers vanished into the morning mist, never to be seen again.

The briar that had choked the Nightwood soon crumbled, and when the robin announced the end of winter, the forest bloomed more splendidly than ever before. An arbor of wild roses grew in the glade where the lovers had first met. There, on the first day of spring, Elaine and Tamlynne were married amidst great rejoicing.